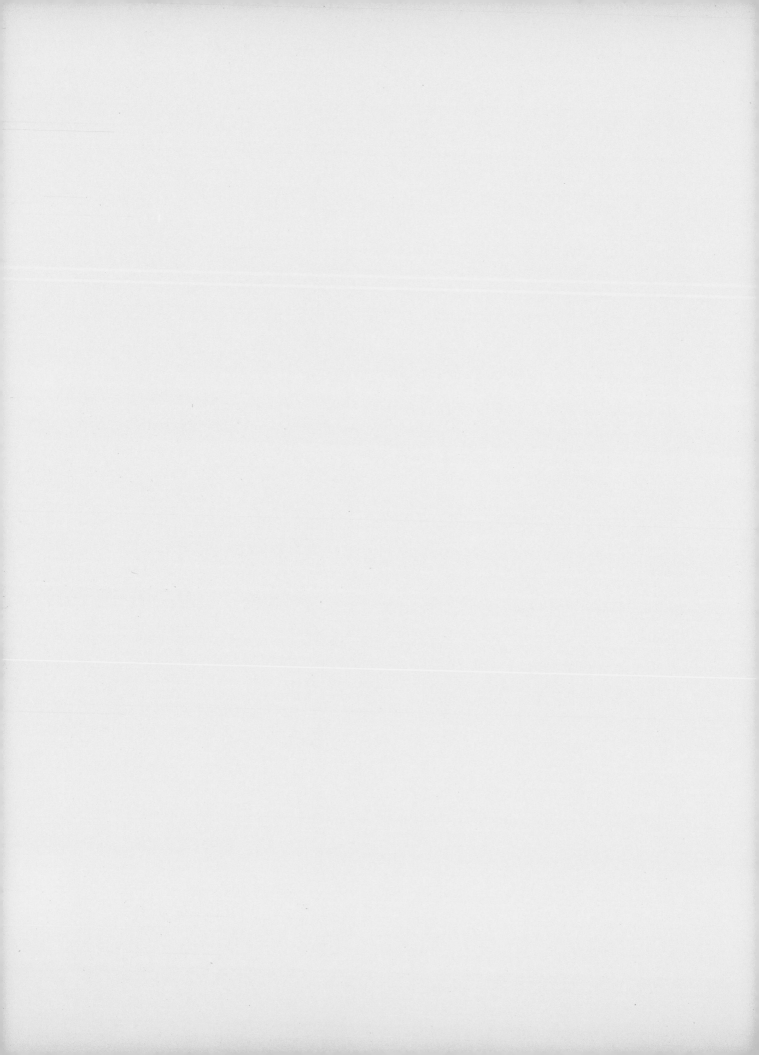

MY GRANDMA'S PHOTOS

MY GRANDMA'S PHOTOS

By Özge Bahar Sunar • Illustrated by Senta Urgan
Translated by Amy Marie Spangler

amazon crossing kids

Text by Özge Bahar Sunar
Illustrations by Senta Urgan
Text and illustrations copyright © 2019 by Kalem Agency
Translation copyright © 2022 by Amy Marie Spangler
The photographs in this book are the property of the author and illustrator and are used with permission.

Previously published as *Anneannemin Fotoğrafları* by Nesin Yayınevi in Turkey in 2019.
Translated from Turkish by Amy Marie Spangler. First published in English by
Amazon Crossing Kids in collaboration with Amazon Crossing in 2022.

Published by Amazon Crossing Kids, New York, in collaboration with Amazon Crossing

www.apub.com

Amazon, Amazon Crossing, and all related logos are trademarks of Amazon.com, Inc., or its affiliates.

ISBN-13: 9781542031158 (hardcover)
ISBN-10: 154203115X (hardcover)

The illustrations were rendered in pastel pencil and collage.

Book design by Tanya Ross-Hughes
Printed in China

First Edition

10 9 8 7 6 5 4 3 2 1

For my grandma, whose love and affection
nurtured me throughout my childhood
—Özge Bahar Sunar

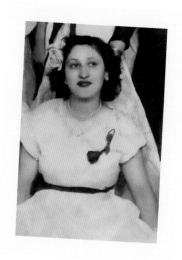

For Raşel, she of the loveliest smile
in all of Yeldeğirmeni . . .
—Senta Urgan

Grandma's ears don't hear very well anymore,
and her eyes aren't what they used to be. . . .

The other day she looked at my doll and asked,
"So you have a new sibling, do you?"

She almost never leaves her armchair.
Most of the time my big sister has to feed her.
Whenever I walk up to her, she's asleep.
Sometimes she gets our names mixed up.

Mom took out some old photos from the wooden trunk.
For some reason they were in black and white.
She placed them in Grandma's hands.
"Do you remember these, Mom?" she asked.

Grandma didn't look at the photos at all.
Her eyes fell shut. She was probably tired again.
Mom got a sad look on her face and walked slowly out of the room.
I stayed with Grandma.

A little while later Grandma woke up.
She glanced over the photos in her hands.
Then holding up one of them, she asked,
"Who's this, Ali? A friend of yours?"

I snuggled up close to her.
I examined the photo carefully,
but I didn't recognize the person in it.
"No," I replied. "I wonder who it is."

Then I noticed the beauty spot on the little girl's cheek.
"I think this is you, Grandma," I said.
"Look at her face and her eyes—they're just like yours.
And she has wavy hair like yours too. . . ."

Grandma peered at the photo.
That, I think, is when her memories came alive.
"Of course I remember that day," she said.
"Oh, how I adored that garden!"

"Look, here's my family and me on a picnic.
And this is the day I married your grandpa!"

"Was everything black and white back then?" I asked.

"No, not at all," Grandma said. "Come, let me show you."
At that moment I felt as if I were being pulled into the photo.
Together with Grandma, I traveled into the past.

Grandma was a child my age now.

"Hurry up, let's go climb the tree in the garden," she said.

I was stunned, seeing my grandma at that age.

Just a moment ago she couldn't even get up out of her chair. . . .

"I'm a child again!" she exclaimed.

She hopped and jumped and laughed joyously.

Grandma climbed nimbly up to the highest branch.

She yelled down to me, "Come on, get up here!"

Taking slow, cautious steps, I climbed up and joined her.

But Grandma—oh, how she leaped from branch to branch!

She showed me how to do it too.

Then she leaned over and whispered in my ear,

"It can't really be taught with words.

You have to find yourself a tree and climb it every day."

abahçe vapurunda

She got down from the tree and began to sprint.
"Wait for me!" I yelled, but she kept going.

Together we leaped into another photo.
Grandma was a young woman now,
enjoying herself on a ferry.
She and her friends were singing.
She had on the most beautiful dress I had ever seen.

I walked up to her and said, "Grandma, you've grown up!"
"Well, my dear Ali, I was a teenager once, too, you know," she said.

Together we tossed pieces of sesame rings at the seagulls.
Then we sat facing the wind and closed our eyes.
"Are we going to sleep now, Grandma?" I asked.
"No," she said. "Now we're going to dream of wonderful things."
"What are you dreaming of, Grandma?" I asked.

Taking my hand, she said, "Come, let me show you."
Then she whisked me off to another memory.

Now Grandma was in a giant shop.
A long, pink measuring tape hung around her neck.
She sewed dresses, skirts, and blouses.
It was the dream she'd had on the ferry: she was making it come true.

"Is this your shop, Grandma?" I asked.
"Yes," she said. "I'm a master seamstress now."
A young woman tried on the skirt Grandma had made for her.
She twirled and laughed, and said she loved it.
Grandma's face beamed proudly, and mine did too.

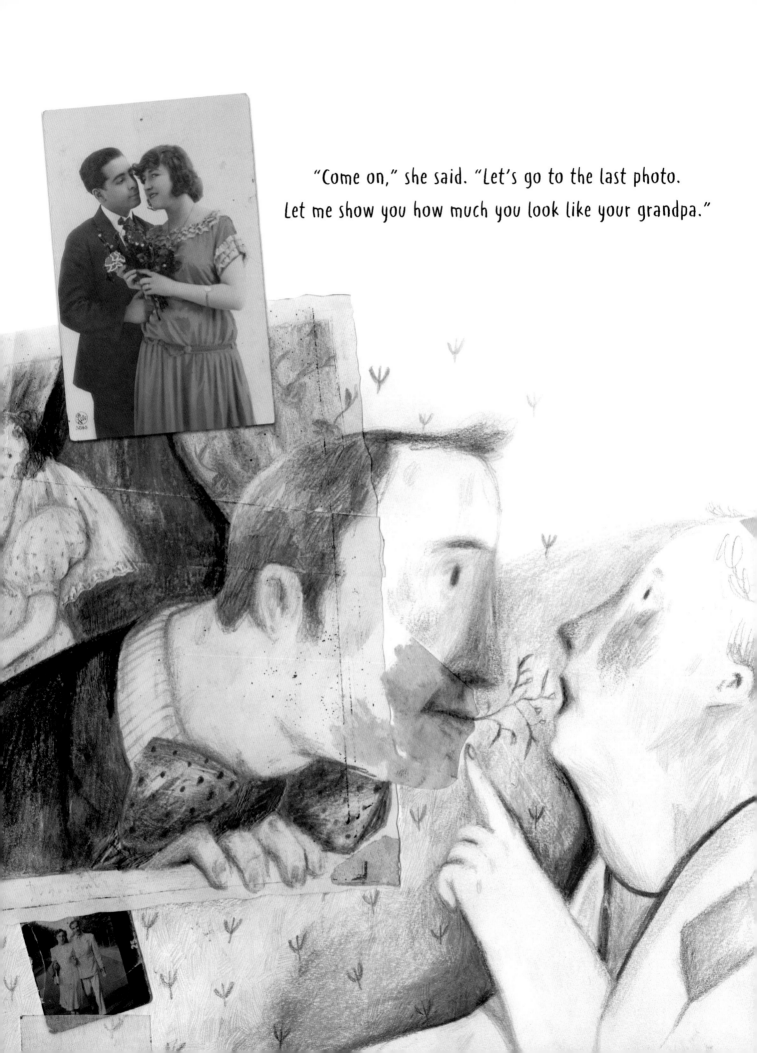

"Come on," she said. "Let's go to the last photo.
Let me show you how much you look like your grandpa."

Now we were at a wedding.
Grandma was the beautiful bride.
She wore a gorgeous wedding gown she'd made herself.
And that handsome man in a suit—that was my grandpa!

I couldn't believe my eyes:
I was watching my grandparents dance on their wedding night!

"All right," she said finally. "It's time for you to go back home."

"But what about you? Aren't you coming?"

"I'm so happy here, my dear little Ali.
I'm going to dance with your grandpa a little longer.
Then maybe we'll visit some other photos.
Your grandpa and I have been apart for such a long time, you know."

"Then I'm going to stay here too.
I'm not going anywhere without you!"

"You have to," she said. "You can't stay here.
You need to collect memories and photos of your own.
If you miss me, I'll be right here, roaming through these photos.
And I won't forget anyone or anything ever again."

I couldn't hold back my tears.
I hugged her tightly again and again before parting.
Then I kissed Grandma one last time.

When I opened my eyes, I was back. . . .

We don't keep Grandma's photos in the trunk anymore.
We've hung most of them on the walls of my room.
Whenever I miss her, I look at her photos.
I'm sure she's still there, at peace, dancing away. . . .